CW00927555

To Jane

Boxes of time

Best wishes

Karal

x

Boxes of time

Karol Darnell

Honesty Press
ESTABLISHED 2022
WWW.HONESTYPRESS.CO.UK

Boxes of time

Photographs: The Darnell collection.
Editing & Formatting: Honesty Press

ISBN: 978-1-7396495-3-1 (Hardcover)
First edition: July 2022 - 10 9 8 7 6 5 4 3 2 1

CONTENTS

The old house

The old house

No one came to the old house now. Ivy grew up the stone walls from the ground to the roof; it twisted its way up the stone mullions furling and wrapping its way up and around the four large square chimneys. The diamond lattice windows too were almost covered, and the tendrils had woven their way through some of the diamond panes, between the glass and the lead, breaking some of them so that the wind would whistle through in the night when only owls and mice were awake.

Angela arrived early; her viewing appointment diary had Mr & Mrs Green in at one o'clock, Mr Webster at three; then Peter Drew at four-thirty. She checked her watch, twelve forty-five. Good, she could sit in the quiet garden in the sunshine and think about what she would say to her clients as they viewed this old property in need of renovation, and fresh to the market that very morning.

The sunshine was warm, Angela spotted an old bench under a large apple tree about ten feet away from what would once have been a sunny terrace, the stone balustrade now covered with ferns and moss with the overgrown branches of shrubs now untamed, lining the path. She started to doze, warmed by the sun, and lulled by the birdsong and peace of the place.

No one came to the old house now. Time had long forgotten the children playing in the garden when nurse would watch over them and the servants scurried to keep the house clean and remaining out of sight of the master. Only cook and Rose remembered how it used to be.

"Rose, Rose! *Where is that girl!*" The old woman shouted. Her voice shrill, echoing through the empty rooms. Angela stirred a little not sure if she had heard anything.

The grass grew thick and unkept, Jones, the gardener had left it to grow, his tired old fingers couldn't hold the tools anymore. He stopped pruning the bushes a very long time ago and yet the roses in the garden continued to bloom, their scent heavy in the air on a still summers evening. The stone garden walls and terraces were now full of weeds where once they were tidied, but Jones left them to grow too. Jones sat in the stone shed with his pipe, watching the garden grow around him. They found him there, on his rickety old chair and they carried him away to the graveyard. No one came to the garden now.

"Rose, Rose! *Where is that girl!*" Angela heard the old woman shouting again. The words drifted away with the wind, lost in the vastness of the empty hallway. Rose couldn't hear; her ears had heard enough, she drifted around in the large old house, going from room to room but no longer having a purpose since the mistress had passed away leaving her with nothing to do.

Her legs were tired and her knees weak from climbing the oak staircase upstairs to the mistress's bedroom. She didn't visit there now. Rose had died many years ago but still the mistress called for her.

"Rose, Rose! *Where is that girl!*" Cook was too far away. She stood with her hands in a large bowl of pastry, sifting the fat and the flour between her fingertips. The pie would need to be in the oven soon for the master's tea. Cook's knurled old fingers, worked almost to the bone. Cook would never hear the mistress shouting; she had passed away and her family collected her short plump body and buried her in her flour dusted apron, a wooden spoon in her hand.

"It's what she would have wanted," they had said as they left her. Nobody paid for a headstone.

"Rose, Rose! *Where is that girl!*" The shouting was loud and shrill, and Angela heard the sound of children's laughter, carried on the wind, lost in the rustling of the trees. The children had grown up now, the two boys gone off to war, never to return and little Emily got married and moved away. Her husband had found her with a noose around her neck, cold and lifeless. Her body brought home and placed in the family vault.

No one came to the old house now. Bats flew in through the open doorway. The solid oak door stood open, its hinges rusted and dry; leaves gathered at the foot of the stairs. No one swept them away anymore and the parquet floor was dense with brown and dried up matter. Even paper cups and crisp packets had blown in on the wind.

"Rose, Rose! *Where is that girl!*" The old woman shouted into the darkness. She was not alone. She could hear footsteps on the staircase and smell the pie in the oven. The smell wafting up to her as it always did, just before teatime. The old woman stood to watch from her window. The garden was neat, Jones was digging over the flowerbed ready for the spring bedding and the children ran around and played hide and seek on the lawn with nurse.

"Rose, Rose! *Where is that girl!*" Angela heard the old woman shouting; but nobody came to the old house now.

Ginny the Gypsy girl

Ginny the gipsy girl

She hadn't wanted to travel alone, but now she had no choice. She couldn't stay here by this brook hidden by trees; the farmer would soon find her, and she had no money to pay him to stay.

She had wanted to set off in the bright sunshine, there were just a few wispy white clouds in the sky and in front of her lay the promise of a warm and calm day. Days like this had been rare this year, and today was the first day all week that she had woken to a bright sky rather than hearing the drumming of the rain on the roof of the caravan.

After drinking a glass of milk and eating the last piece of bread, she sat cross legged on the grass, face turned to the sun, breathing slowly - in through her nose and out through the pursed lips of her mouth. The horse greeted her with a whinny, but she didn't look at him. Two ash trees above her stood proud and full at last. The feather like leaves reaching out their long fingers, rustling in the gentle breeze; William Morris patterned against the blue of the sky. Seeds hung like bunches of grapes on the south facing side of the tree, as if waiting to swell and ripen in the summer sunshine, a dream of wine making that will never come to pass. Long twisted branches, no longer stark as they had been all winter, were now verdant and green; heavy with life and the ivy twisted trunks, dark and thick blocking out the light to the ground below. Two wood pigeons cooed their romantic intentions, flapping noisily in their attempts at clumsy lovemaking, distracting her as she tried to focus on her breathing.

Once she felt calm enough to continue with her day, she started to pack her few belongings away and untied Baxter from the tree behind her. Somehow, he had managed to wrap his rope twice around it and the stupid thing hadn't been able to get at any fresh grass this morning.

"Stupid horse," she said to him. "We'll be late setting off now." She tossed him some hay and placed his feed bucket under his nose, not caring too much when he tipped it over in his eagerness to eat. It had never mattered to Jim what time they set off, or even whether they did or not. Jim would only move camp if Baxter chose to walk. Many times, he would just stand nuzzling Jim, and refusing to move; dozing until he decided to oblige.

She remembered some of Jim's last words to her, "look after Baxter for me Ginny, he's a smart horse, gypsy bred he is."

Seventeen years her senior, it had been love at first sight, a matching of minds and life objectives, a wonderful mix of humour, laughter, and passion. Four whole years of her life had passed her by in what seemed like a matter of weeks, yet it was all she could remember as if time had stood still; four years of being a wanderer, living life as a gypsy; but now he was gone, and she had to journey alone. The problem was, she didn't know where she was going. Where Jim went, she followed. He never stated a destination or appeared to have planned where they were headed, that was decided by Baxter, but when they arrived at a place, Jim would say, "I always wanted to visit here," and he would smile contentedly, pat Baxter on the neck, and everything was alright.

Today Ginny managed to harness Baxter and he obliged by backing between the shafts as if he at least knew where they were headed.

"We have to go south, Baxter," She whispered into his ear. "South, do you understand?"

Jim had said very little about the place they were headed, but now he was dead. His life was ended before they had expected, and she would now have to travel alone. She remembered his words; he had told her many times of his dream but never told her where it was.

"We will be safe there Ginny. We can live in peace and never need for anything. We will have shelter and our own land to live on. We can grow crops and never be hungry."

But now he was at the end, far sooner than the doctor had said, six weeks transpired to be only six days.

"Just three words - three words Ginny…" he mumbled.

"What three words?" she begged. "Jim tell me please, what are the words. Where is it?"

The gurgling in his throat was getting worse and she had struggled to hear his voice above the sound of the wind in the trees.

"Loyal.home.tr…"
He breathed one last time, and he was gone.

Carnac

Carnac

This wasn't the first time that Bryn had visited Carnac, he had been here many times as a young man; his university degree in archaeology being the background to an interest in prehistory that never waned as the years flew by. The sun glinted on his camera lens as he framed the shot, capturing the standing stones, the menhir alignments that stretched away as far as the eye could see; and his wife to give perspective. There since the dawn of time these giant megalithic stones intrigued him. Their reasons for being there and the meanings that the ancestors had for erecting them made him question even the experts' explanations. He queried them, choosing to touch the stones, trying to hear into the past, but they did not give away their secrets to him. Why should they?

Turning to follow his wife, he almost didn't see the small boy sat at the entrance to the dolmen. His hair unkempt with just a tunic covering his slight body, he looked straight back at Bryn and in that split second their eyes met, and the boy was gone. Bryn blinked and looked around again, disbelieving his own eyes he called his wife.

'Kath, come back here. Did you see that boy?'

She walked back slowly not listening nor answering his question.

'What now, I've seen them Bryn, we've been here for long enough. Let's go to get some coffee.'

She started to walk away from him again and down the hillside into the woodland that led back to the car park.

The smell of pine and gorse filled the air, the sound of the forest birds, shrill and loud in the peace of the place. Cricket's chirping. A church bell tolled from the nearby village, a steady dong, dong, dong; muffled yet clear, perhaps ringing out for the new

King, proclaiming the death of the old Queen at home in England.

She watched as a man appeared, he walked silently through the coppice of trees, he was strangely dressed in an animal skin. He held a spear in his right hand. His grey hair and beard framing his younger face. Something about his smile made her quiver as she passed him, she smiled back and turned to watch him walk away but he was gone. She walked on along the path, woodland sounds echoed in the deep silence, a cacophony of sound.

Bryn hurried after her, 'did...did you see that man?' he said, confusion etched upon his face. 'Where did he go?'

Kate smiled slowly, 'don't you know, Bryn? You've studied history all your life, don't you know the past when you see it?'

Gone fishing

Gone fishing

"Just along here, not too far now" Rob said as the three boys walked over the open field towards the river. "I know a great place; the water is quite shallow, and you can see the fish in the water from the old bridge."

"This bag is heavy," complained Mike.

"Stop grouching!"

"Why do I have to carry it?" he grumbled.

"Because you said you would. I've got the flask of coffee and the sandwiches."

"It's getting colder, I hope it doesn't rain," said Ben. We only have one umbrella."

"And that's mine!" laughed Rob. "You two will have to get wet. Down here," Rob disappeared into the thicket at the edge of the river, the other two boys followed carefully behind, wary to not slip down the steep slope to the water. Finally, they reached the riverbank and a small bend in the river afforded them a grassy banking to sit on and a gravel beach.

"It's a great place Rob," Ben agreed. "You were right after all."

"Yeah, usually you get it wrong, and we end up in a rubbish place and never catch anything." griped Mike as he slid the heavy bag from his shoulder.

"Put the keep nets over there and pass me that bait box," said Ben, eager to start fishing. He beckoned to Rob who was unpacking his tackle and his foldable fishing stool while Mike stretched his back, hands on his hips.

"Is that your radio I can hear Rob, turn it off, I don't want to listen to your rubbish music while I'm fishing." he whinged again.

"I haven't brought it," replied Rob. "Must be some other people further up the river."

"They must be coming this way, it's getting louder."

"It's a drum. I don't like drums."

"It sounds like a marching band. Where's that coming from?" Rob questioned standing up to look around.

"We're away from the road here. The old bridge is just behind those trees but there's no road to it now."

The sound of the drumming grew louder. A steady drum beat of two marching drums, Tara, tara, tara, ta ta, and the sound of many heavy boots marching. The boys looked around and then at each other.

"They're going towards the bridge," Ben said, scurrying back up the slope to where he could see the old bridge. "There's no one there!" he shouted back to the others.

"It's getting louder, it'll frighten the fish away and then we'll catch nothing." Mike moaned, following his mate up the slope to stand beside him surveying the field where the noise was coming from.

"Where? I can't see anything."

"Sounds like they're coming closer. What's that smell? Like fireworks?"

BANG, BANG! Both boys jumped as they heard a volley of musket fire accompanied by men shouting.

'Gunpowder! It's gunpowder, look over there!" A whisp of smoke floated above the bridge and a clashing of steel against steel and gunshots rang out as if a skirmish were taking place in front of them, yet the boys could see nothing.

Ben ran towards the old bridge, the sound of fighting and shouting grew louder, the smell of gunpowder and clashing of the ram rods as the men reloaded their muskets.

"Take aim! FIRE!" came the command.

The gunfire echoed around and the yells of the men fighting was shrill on the air. The three friends could hear the crashing of battle, men fighting and shrieking, and combat everywhere. The pungent smell of gunpowder and smoke surrounded them. The bridge was empty.

"Where are they?" shouted Rob, spinning around, searching for the origin of the battle noise. They were in the middle of the bridge now, the clamour and racket encompassing them, the smoke and noise of battle loud in their ears. There was gruesome yell and a loud splash behind them, as if a man had fallen from the bridge into the water below them.

They ran to the parapet and looked over, expecting to see what they could hear; a man flailing about in the deep water. The noises subsided and the drumbeat grew more distant as they heard the men march away again.

"Where is he?"

The boys looked down into the undisturbed stillness of the river, gazing in disbelief as they watched the fishes swim peacefully and gracefully away.

No train

No train

I looked at the timetable on the wall of the train station waiting room. A young man in ripped, dirty jeans and torn tee-shirt sat opposite me, he grinned a toothless smile at me, a scar on his face still dripping blood.

"There won't be any trains today," he said rather quietly. He looked a little dazed drawing on his cigarette and blowing the smoke into the middle of the little room.

I sat down on the wooden bench without answering him and reached into my bag for my book and tried to ignore him. I took a quick glance at the station clock; only quarter past two, I had half an hour to wait for my train, the 14:45 to Aberystwyth.

"I said there are no trains!" he repeated.

"Yes… I know, I can wait," I answered him trying to avoid his wide-eyed stare. I opened my book and started to read. I couldn't catch up with my story and so I flicked back a couple of pages to remind myself what had happened.

"No trains at all!" finally he stood up and walked over to me. "I said no trains!" he looked over the top of my book and shouted, "NO TRAINS!"

"I'm… I'm sorry." I stuttered, finally looking at him. "You didn't make sense, why? when is the next train?"

"Cancelled! Accident near Craven Arms, many people die. Track will have to be repaired."

"How do you know this?" There was a bruise and a lump on his forehead. "And... why are you sitting here then?"

"Here to warn you," he said before walking back to where he had been sitting.

"When was this?" I asked, starting to panic. "When was the accident?"

He looked down at his watch and paused before answering. "Half past two!"

A babble of young girls entered the waiting room, laughing and joking between themselves. They looked at me and then over to the dishevelled man.

"No trains!" he repeated to them. They continued to laugh and talk over him until he stood up and shouted in a very loud voice. "NO BLOODY TRAINS! NO BLOODY TRAINS!"

One of the girls turned to her friends, shrugging her shoulders before they all sat down and continued to chatter loudly.

I looked at my watch; Twenty past two it read. I checked the station clock again, I was right, twenty past two.

"Did you say half past two?" I asked above the din the girls were making. "But it's only twenty past two." I checked my mobile, 14:21 the screen confirmed.

"Two thirty. Accident!" He took out another cigarette and slowly lit it. His hand trembled. "It hasn't happened yet."

I rose from my seat and headed to the door onto the platform. I ran towards the booking office where a bespectacled lady sat in her little cubicle.

"There's going to be an accident!" I cried at her. "Stop the train!"

"I can't do that! Why?" she asked, taking in my shocked face.

"The two forty-five! It will crash at half past two at Craven Arms!"

She looked up at the clock and then back down at her desk, ignoring me. My heart was pounding now, I turned to run in slow motion down the platform to a station guardsman.

As I ran, I looked over to my left, into the waiting room; the girls and the man had gone.

The gossamer veil

The gossamer veil

Eoine woke from her long sleep. Her baby stirred beside her. Her man did not wake, his gentle breath calm in the still of the early morning. The baby snuffled, his tiny mouth searched for her nipple, and she felt him begin to feed.

Peace surrounded her, their bed of moss and bracken soft and warm beneath her. The timber roof of the roundhouse, high above her keeping out the light and wind; keeping out the world outside. This was her place, her belonging and where she yearned to be once more.

She remembered her baby and the love of her man, a good hunter, and his protection, so solid in her memory.

But this waking was not the one she dreamed of. This waking was the lonely one she did not want. This waking was the one of death, from the long vigil, from the long night of the past.

They had come, fierce and murderous from the South. They had come one night to take the hill; to steal away their Dobunni land and their lives. Many men battled at the gate, slaughtered, and left to rot, their blood seeping into the land of their fathers. Women had screamed in terror, blind panic scattering them like spilt grain. They had come with fire, burning down their homes, the thick acrid smoke clogging the air with the smell of burning flesh.

They had killed her man and her child. He had fallen over her to protect her as she cradled their child in her arms; a spear in his back and their child crushed beneath her. No cries now; they were gone, and she was alone.

She stood on the deserted hillside at dawn, the silken thread of a spider's web spun across the doorway to the roundhouse of her dream. It was done, the long nights vigil for the dead.

Eoine would wake once every year on this morning when the celebration of the New Year dawned, and the old year died. She blinked in the morning sunlight, yellow primroses under her bare feet, soft as she walked on the grass. Bluebells would be blooming in the woods below the ramparts and the blossom would be covering the trees. All was quiet in the early morning as if the world was at peace and her family were sleeping still.

Skylarks trilled above her in the cloudless sky and a gentle breeze blew; warmth from the sun touched her bare shoulder but Eoine shuddered and covered herself with her shawl.

They were here again. Each year they came, different people in strange clothes. They spoke loudly in tongues she did not understand.

They couldn't see her; they talked and didn't know she was there. Over the years there were some quiet, contemplative souls who must have seen her. They must have heard her crying. These people smiled at her as if they saw her, but their smiles passed through her.

Many years passed and each time she woke she saw changes. She gazed from the hill and across the vastness stretching below her in every direction. What was once marshland and forest, one great space was now a patchwork, divided into pieces; some yellow, some green, some still wooded where the roe deer hid. Great squares of colour where food now grew and where herds of animals grazed. The Avon water, a great and powerful river, diverted by man now yet still weaving its course across the land to the north of the hill; from where the sun rose to where it set; and where the water gods played and some years sent great floods to spread across the land, turning the green fields into great lakes.

Trees were felled and great castles and timber houses were built. Spires and towers for the new religion, stone-built churches were erected in the old and sacred places. She watched as they built great buildings, towns, and villages for more people to live in. She observed as large armies marched across the land and she witnessed battles, and plagues, and she watched as the people died.

Each year Eoine would wake from her vigil for her man and her child. Each year was a little different. Sometimes rain would batter the hillside and she would stand alone in the wind. Watching; waiting.

There were huge beasts that flew along on great rails and other great birds that flew in the air in straight lines, scratching the sky.

Noise, and speed, and terror.

Eoine watched as new families came and went, but they only visited when the sun shone, they didn't live up here. Some came with wheels and others with large packs on their backs with food to eat together. Some would walk away as fast as they came but some would linger, laying on the soft grass at her feet, dozing in the tranquillity of the lazy afternoon sun.

Poets and artists would dream, and some would bring music in small boxes and not hear the music of the hillside at all.

Eoine watched and she waited until the sun dipped behind the hill to the west and all the people left her. The earth cooled again with the evening breeze, and she would enter her home to lie once again on her bed of moss, covered with fur and she would sleep once more.

The gossamer thread of time weaved its veil, shimmering and glinting to those who dare to see.

The children

The children

The crackling and spitting of the logs on the open fire, lulled him as he sat in his wing backed leather chair. His unlit pipe held loosely between his yellowing teeth. The nicotine had stained his greying moustache too, adding a splash of ginger colour to his pale features. He stared at his brown tweed slippers, where his big toe had finally managed to rub away the fabric and peep through. His tartan dressing gown stained and well-worn yet still comfortable after all these years, fell open to expose his dirty blue pinstriped pyjamas beneath.

"Bah!" He didn't like children and they were here again. Running up and down the long corridor upstairs. He could hear their heavy footsteps as they chased each other up and down, the girls giggling and the whoops and cheers of the boys were getting louder every time they visited.

He leaned forwards to pick up his tobacco pouch, it was almost empty. "Bah!" He grumbled again as he pinched together the small amount of tobacco with his thin fingers. Holding his pipe with the other hand, he placed the tobacco in it and deftly struck the match, sucking on his pipe in a well-practiced routine. The tobacco smouldered and as he breathed out through his nose and pursed thin lips, the smoke escaped and filled the space, slowly weaving its way around his head.

Rubbing the white whiskers on his chin and slowly puffing on his pipe, old Mr Prendergast closed his eyes and dozed.

Upstairs the children were silent again. He could only hear them when he was awake and now, they were hushed. Soundless and noiselessly Emily picked up her doll. Carys and James sat in the corner near the top of the stairs and little Johnny stared out of the cracked and dirty window to the garden below. The snow was falling again, but the children couldn't go outside to play like they used to. Their memories of life were distant now. Recollections of a childhood, long gone and stolen from them. Emily had been only five when she had died, her frail little body, wracked by a cough until she slowly faded away one January, when the snow was falling, and the fire had been lit to keep her cold body warm.

James and Johnny had perished, tragically one winters day while out skating on the glassy surface of the frozen pond. The ice splintered and gave way beneath them with a large crack! Neither of the brothers could swim.

Carys, a little older than the others, orphaned as a baby yet still a child, had been brought in as a scullery maid at the age of ten. Her job of taking out the ashes and laying the fires each morning sadly being the end of her, as the smouldering ashes in the pan she was carrying suddenly burst into flames when a gust of wind from the open window lifted the sparks, poor Cary's pinafore caught light, and the flames engulfed her.

Now they would only play when the old man was listening. They were waiting for him. It would not be long now and soon the children would creep downstairs to look at his aged face, wrinkly and tired. Mr Prendergast stirred in his sleep. He heard them whispering in his ear, chattering.

"Come with us Billy," whispered Emily. "Come and play with us in the garden."

"It's snowing, come outside." tempted Johnny. The old man tried to push the wispy feint figures of the children away, his arms waving out blindly. He opened his eyes, they were becoming stronger, he could see them more clearly now.

"Bah! Go away, leave me alone." he shouted, hitting out at them. The children faded away, their voices retreating upstairs, and all was quiet again.

Monkey Doo

Monkey Doo

Crafted from clay, his tunic glazed with cobalt blue and iron yellow; the figurine of a monkey in tribal dress held one arm high as if looking out into the future. In his other hand, he held his ancestral spear. Sturdy black boots marching him through time.

Monkey Doo had travelled far, and many years had passed. A warrior on one of Hannibal's elephants once carried him carefully across the Alps wrapped in a blanket in sturdy panniers. He protected the warrior, healing him of his wounds more than once and although many of the elephants and soldiers had died on that journey, his guardian had kept him safe until one night he was spirited away by a roman soldier trying his luck.

Evil befell those with malicious intent, and the roman soldier drowned. His abandoned bag was discovered by a rock on the edge of the river by a poor yet beautiful servant girl. She so admired the blue of Monkey Doo's tunic and placed him high on a shelf in her humble home. Once he had seen her safely married to a kind and rich husband, Monkey Doo found a new home with a traveller, who found his fortune when his carpentry skills were praised and much sought after in towns and villages on his journey west.

Centuries passed and Monkey Doo journeyed on, changing hands when his spells were cast and whosoever looked kindly on Monkey Doo, prospered. Those possessors who protected and admired him, came to no harm and each one soon flourished before Monkey Doo moved on once more. Another Roman soldier bade goodbye to his family and marched to Britain to help build Hadrian's wall with Monkey Doo safely packed away in a wooden trunk. By some misfortune, the roman gambolled away his satchel and Monkey Doo could not help him when the battle came, and the poor soldier perished, as did the man who won the bet; this was not the type of owner that Monkey Doo wanted to assist.

On one occasion he was lot number 231 in a house clearance auction, and he watched as the bidders vied with each other to own him. He looked around the room until he spotted his next custodian raise his tentative hand after a nudge from his excited wife.

"Sold." The gavel hit the block with a resounding crack and Monkey Doo was taken to a small, terraced house in the middle of a busy city. Her uncle had been ill for some time, but neither of them had expected to be benefactors in his will. They moved shortly afterwards into a large country estate with a swimming pool and servants too. Far too fine now to need a small ceramic statue with a monkey's face and a need now to move on again.

The antique shop was dark at the back and high up on a shelf, Monkey Doo hid, covered in dust. He was waiting for his next inheritor, one who would treasure him and needed his magic once more.

"I'm not sure of his age," the shop owner said as he lifted Monkey Doo down from the high shelf and handed him to Paula.

"Byzantine perhaps or maybe a 1970's art college project. I don't know to be honest, but he's yours for twenty quid."

Paula caressed the statuette and gazed into Monkey Doo's eyes. She was sure she saw it blink as she handed over her money. She gently wrapped her new ornament in her cardigan placing him safely into her bag, then continued to her hospital appointment. Once safely at home she placed Monkey Doo on top of her bookcase and waited for her husband to return from work to tell him the wonderful news that she was completely cancer free.

That evening when Paula's niece called to tell them that she had finally found a flat, hoping that she would get the job offer in the post within the week. Monkey Doo stirred once more.

"Can I have him Aunty P?" Dawn asked looking up at the figure on top of the bookcase. "Please, he's the same colour as the curtains in my bedroom."

Monkey Doo blinked. Time to move on' he thought.

La Ria

La Ria

'Yoda II' is Vincent's boat. The white one with the big black engine. This is what the neighbour had said when he quizzed her on her relationship to the family and her reason for being in their house. Her schoolgirl French relaying the story of how they had been friends for most of her life and that she met Valérie on a beach in Cornwall as children. He told her how his grandfather, Monsieur Joannic, had taught Vincent to fish as a very young boy. But she knew this already, the memories were part of her, this place was her past too.

She lay in her bed that first morning listening to the familiar chink, chink of the sailboat rigging ringing against the masts, and the slap, slap of the water under the hulls of the little boats as they bobbed about at the edge of the river at high tide. The warp ropes tight as the strings on a violin, waiting for the musician to pull the bow to create beautiful music.

The smell of oil paint, warmed by the morning sunshine, wafted through the house, warm, pleasant and such a feature of home.

The painter was still here, his work covering the walls, the old tuna fishing boats, and the carcasses of ships past, the river that he loved, paintings of his family, the violist, the cellist, and so many more. His familiar style exuding the passion and love of his craft. The colours, strong and vibrant, just as he was.

"Papa ! je peux aller pêcher ?"

The sound of the child's voice wafted faintly up to her ears above the roar of the river as the tide turned and the strong current noisily dragged the water away, under the bridge towards the sea. Swirling with white froth as it rounded the jagged rocks, fierce whirlpools tumbling the water in its race to empty the Ria. A couple of hours had passed; she had eaten her baguette, drinking English tea, watching as the seaweed covered rocks reappeared and the boats rested at last on the sand in front of the house. Their ropes relaxed now, at rest once more.

From here she could see all that she remembered. The strong force of the river, the bridge, and the pretty white Breton cottages. Motorboats battled against the strong currant and men stood on the jetty, their fishing rods angled, waiting for the first bite and catch of the day. Little had changed; the apple tree had grown, throwing the apples to land with a thud on the grass below; some stored in a crate by the garden door where the painter once worked, his brushes in his hand, his palette knife skilfully scratching the canvas as he created his oil painting. In the garden, memories of parents and grandparents, watching the children play while they drank tea brought as a gift from England. A mix of English and French conversation drifting on the wind as they caught up on their gossip and sea birds added their voices too.

"Papa," the child's voice, stronger now. "Regarde mon poisson, et les crevettes, Papa !"

Again, the sound of the past, clear, and strong; distant but not forgotten. The children's voices would always be heard in the quiet if she listened with her heart and it will always be summer here. The children will bring their children and the future will unfold just as they had planned.

A morning swim would restore her, and the water was warmer than she remembered, but it was just as clear. She could see the tiny fishes and shrimp dart away as she walked further into the water. Two small crab scurried under a small rock for safety. Strips of seaweed strung like ribbons and lace on a washing line, blowing in a submerged world. She plunged under the glassy surface of the water reaching out with her arms and legs in a positive breaststroke, her muscles stretching for the first time in ages as she took her first swim of the holiday. Later they would eat thick slices of ham and salad with bread and cheeses, as they always used to do; her fathers' favourite too and she smiled to remember his love of all things French...of holiday...of life itself.

An hour in the sunshine, alone with her thoughts but surrounded by the love of her friends, was the perfect way to pass an hour until lunchtime. Her book lay on the grass underneath the apple tree, and she placed her towel on a lounger and started to read. How could she concentrate? With the smell of the river, the blue of the water; the perfect blue, a blue he captured so well in his paintings. How? with the voices from the present mingling so well with the distant voices from the past in a timeless music that she could listen to forever. An orchestra of sounds on the warm September breeze.

And what was it about a tablecloth on a balcony, overlooking the sea, that was so typically French? Or an egret, poised upon a rock that captured the attention of those who sat at that table? An instant in time, a piece of life that, although repeated many times, was just such a perfect moment to savour as if it would never be the same again.

Nothing would ever be the same again. Our fathers were gone, our mothers now elderly, and our children grown with lives of their own. There were to be no regrets, just many great and lasting memories and now the chance to make more. A boat trip to the beach later would be the perfect opportunity, except that the weather has broken and is cooler today. That is the climate here. It can rain further along the coast, but still be sunny here, the sea air blowing inland and banishing any more rain clouds, it would not be long before the sun broke through the grey clouds and warm her as she waited for the others. A unique microclimate and perfect to do something whatever the weather. The fish are still jumping, the fishermen in their little boats continue to battle the strong current. The smell of fresh bread. The ticking away of time, not by a clock but by the work that needs to be done.

The crashing waves of the Atlantic Ocean at the mouth of the estuary, always so savage and wild and free. She turned to gaze out over the sea, the spray fresh on her face against the wind. La barre d'Etel, was always impressive. She remembered the battle of the tunny fishing boats of her youth as they faced the wide ocean after leaving the safety of the harbour, their bravery and skill in navigating the sandbank, the long poles that held their fishing nets slowly lowered into the sea as they faced the night ocean of black.

The tunny fishing boats from long ago were now gone, their carcasses resting like discarded fish bones in small coves along the riverbank, between the rocks and only visited by painters when the water is low, or the fish at high tide. Jacques came here too, and the past was recorded in blues and green, red, and ochre on his canvas.

But the Ria is not just water with its ever-changing colours from gentle blue to deep forbidding grey. Silver, placid pools where the oysters grow; and violent tumbling whirlpools bringing and taking the tide and the fish, crabs, and lobster. There is so much more to the Ria than water; there are vast woodlands, small villages and abandoned cottages nestled among the many tributaries. The Ria, stretching its fingers deep into the countryside, crooked and twisted like an old mans crippled fingers after a lifetime fishing or tilling the plough. This year the trees inland are dry, despite the life-giving water of the river, this year there was very little rainfall, and the undergrowth is crisp and brown already. Dried ferns and autumn leaves shrivelled before their time, holly berries, red now in preparation for winter. Autumn has arrived too soon, the usual slow creep into winter is somehow speeded up as if there is a race to die, to shrivel too soon where once there was a slow, paced reluctance into the autumn. The holding back of life in a slow and ordered pace had been lost this year with the long, hot summer.

She listened to the rustling leaves, the swirling treetops dancing in the air, high up against the sky and the cry of birds screeching like witches as the sun glinted on the retreating tide leaving mudflats and stranded creatures for their banquet. Valérie told her that she imagined fairies here and water nymphs, and in the quiet magic of the forest, she also believed they were there, peeping through the thickets, their laughter tinkling in the air as they played their games in the deepness of the woodland. There was also still the pleasure of taking a rest after their long walk along the twisting woodland paths, of lying on a floating pontoon with her feet in the water, listening to the estuary birds shriek as they dip and dive.

She had almost forgotten the street markets, the vast choice of fresh fruit and vegetables on offer. The poissonnière, charcutier and boulangère; all trades that survive in every town and village in France but not many to be found in England anymore. She filled her basket far more than she would at home, buying with her memories of taste rather than out of necessity. It would all be eaten, the peaches and tomatoes, soft and ripe and sweet, crusty bread and all manner of cheeses and sliced meats, all far tastier than in England and she once more wondered why she lived there at all anymore. Langoustine and crab, vivant and delicious with just a touch of mayonnaise was the perfect choice for lunch. She would swim again after eating. There was always time for another swim, irresistible and therapeutic, the turquoise and green of the Ria, beckoning her once more into the fresh and gentle water.

Feathered wisps of clouds brushing the bright blue of the sky as if they were gentle brush strokes, tentatively placed on a new canvas.

Time now and time then are the same, as if it were the same time. The same space in life and being. Once in this place she was always here. She would always be here as if time were one continuum. A continuous loop of memory and of existence. The past and present meshes into one - always. Marie-Claire stands on her balcony and the children play. She was once again young, and the future would yet unfold before her.

The Goom Stool

The Goom Stool

The air was sweet with the smell of dry grass, the high summer heat warming the tarmac road as she walked. Twigs cracked underfoot as she climbed over the style from the road, dropping her down into the cool shade of the footpath that led through the small copse of trees to lead out across the open field further along. Lisa adjusted her small rucksack, feeling the sweat run down her back as she lifted the weight of it away from her. She scanned the wide field in front of her for the footpath and headed off towards a large oak tree that stood at the far corner. Two roe deer sprang from the safety of the hedge, startled by her presence. They leapt away, their heads held high as they momentarily stopped to survey her from a safe distance, their noses absorbing the scent on the warm breeze. As she reached the brow of the hill she stood in the shade of the old oak, looking out over the cornfield that had been freshly mown.

The grain had been harvested, leaving neat rows of straw shimmering on the ground before her. She walked a few more steps to the first row of yellow straw, piled as if ready to be spun into golden thread by Rumpelstiltskin in the much-loved children's story. She dropped to her knees and shrugged off her heavy pack, retrieving from it her last can of cider, which was decidedly warm now as she drained the contents. The softness of the straw beckoned, and she lay down to rest for a while, the smell, sweet as she lay back into its softness. Such a cosy bed indeed.

The heat of the sun, intense before the next fluffy cloud scudded across the sky to cover it for a few seconds before sailing away again to leave the heat from the sun to burn into her skin. A buzzard cried, circling overhead.

She hadn't been aware that she had fallen asleep, but she awoke to the sound of cheering in the village in the valley below the hill. She dusted off the pieces of straw, fishing bits of it from her hair as she looked around. The straw now stood in stooks around her although she hadn't remembered seeing any when she lay down.

Hoisting her bag to her shoulders she started to walk towards the bottom corner of the field to where she had seen the footpath sign earlier.

Looking around puzzled as it didn't appear to be there anymore; a withy gate hung where she recalled there being a style the last time that she had walked this way. She crossed the small common, the bracken thick and abundant at this time of year, to drop down where the new houses had been built only the year before, the locals were furious.

The cheering sounded louder now as she walked along the cobbled path towards the village, but the new houses were not there. She passed by the oddly named "Goom Stool Cottage", the name had always intrigued her but today as she rounded the corner, the shouting became louder and the full horror of the origin of the name of the cottage came into view.
Whooping and cheering came from the villagers, who were strangely dressed in peasant clothing, homespun

skirts and men in britches and tall hats. She watched in dismay as an old woman, tied to a chair on the end of a long pole was plunged into the village pond.

Laughter and jeers taunted the poor woman as she came up, gasping for breath before being ducked under the water again.

"She hexed my cow!" shouted one man while more cries of "she's a witch, duck her again!" rose from the angry mob.

Lisa ran forwards.

"Stop!" she shouted. "Stop, what are you doing?" The crowd ignored her as if she wasn't there.

"Help me, Lisa!" the poor woman yelled, looking straight at her. Lisa ran through the mob towards the woman tied to the ducking stool. She caught her gaze as she spluttered once more, gasping for air, spitting green water out of her mouth.

"Stop!" Lisa screamed again, turning to face the swarm of angry people as she reached the edge of the pool; but they were gone. She swung back round to look for the woman, but she was nowhere to be seen either.

Cackling, caught by a strong gust rippling through the leaves of the trees, and the shrieking of the peasants was carried away upon it.

Dancing and leaping, darting high and then low,
The flickering flames cast their shadowy glow
On the petrified children with fear in their faces,
Whilst the witch with her broomstick, up and down
paces.

Wind and the rain blowing through the old doorway,
Broken and battered for many a long day,
The creaking of trees in the forest so deep,
Wolves wailing and howling, and no one can sleep.

This broken-down house, deserted and old,
Makes the flesh creep and the sweat to run cold,
The shrill whistle of bats swooping down from the wall
Just miss my head, and I feel myself fall.

Falling, down to the depths of a bottomless pit,
The thoughts and the visions now all seem to fit,
For here I lay waken. Cold! Dazed! and I seem
To be lay on the floor. For t'was only a dream.

Brian Darnell
1937-2018

Karol has always been an avid reader and lover of words, writing poetry and short stories for her own amusement. Her first novel *'Don't miss the last train home'* has been very well received and a further novel is in the pipeline.
Details to follow on the publisher's website - www.honestypress.co.uk
This collection of short stories will hopefully make you; the reader think about how we perceive time and who lives in it.